MAMA'S
KISS

Mama's kisses to Heidi, Adam, Jason, Betsy, and Joanne;
Grandmama's kisses to Glendon, Maddison, Alison, David,
Caroline, and Amelia —J.Y.

To Halliday and Abigail, xo —D.B.

Text © 2008 by Jane Yolen.
Illustrations © 2008 by Daniel Baxter.

Handprint Books is an imprint of Chronicle Books LLC.

Book design by NeuStudio.
Typeset in Mrs. Eaves.
Manufactured in China.

Library of Congress Cataloging-in-Publication Data
Yolen, Jane.
Mama's kiss / by Jane Yolen ; illustrations by Daniel Baxter.
p. cm.
"Handprint books."
Summary: A kiss from Mama misses its intended target and instead embarks
on a merry adventure as it slips, slides, and twists its way around the world.
ISBN 978-0-8118-6683-5
[1. Stories in rhyme. 2. Kissing—Fiction.] I. Baxter, Daniel, 1965– ill. II. Title.
PZ8.3.Y76Ma 2008
[E]—dc22
2008021177

10 9 8 7 6 5 4 3 2 1

Chronicle Books LLC
680 Second Street, San Francisco, California 94107

www.chroniclekids.com

MAMA'S KISS

by Jane Yolen

illustrations by Daniel Baxter

Handprint Books

an imprint of
chronicle books · san francisco

Mama smiles and throws me kisses,

Most land right, but one kiss misses.

Mama says she'll throw another,

It sails off toward Baby Brother.

Baby burps, the kiss goes wide,

Through the window and outside.

He spins around.
The kiss then goes . . .

Catches Dog upon the nose,

. . . and smacks Cat who climbs a tree,

Where the kiss bumps into Honey Bee.

Bee flies off. She's looking funny.

Leaves the kiss stuck in her honey.

Bear comes by and with his paw
Sticks the kiss upon his jaw.

Gives the kiss, with bear-hug tight,
To his missus—such delight!

She goes back into their lair,

Where the kiss is grabbed
by Baby Bear.

On his thumb, into his mouth,
He sneezes big—that kiss goes south!

Lands upon a runner's hair,
As he hurries past the lair,
Jogging home to help his wife,
The one he's loved for his whole life.

Mama tucks us kids in bed.
The kiss slides off my Mama's head . . .

. . . and bounces off my cheek instead!

Kiss!
Kiss!
Here it is!

A kiss can go the world around,
And come back where it should be found.